THE ROOSTER PRINCE
Retold by Sydell Waxman
Illustrated by Giora Carmi

PITSPOPANY

NEW YORK ◆ JERUSALEM

Published by Pitspopany Press
Text Copyright © 2000 by Sydell Waxman
Illustrations Copyright © 2000 by Giora Carmi

Design: Tiffen Studios (T.C. Peterseil)

PITSPOPANY PRESS books may be purchased for educational or
special sales by contacting:

        Marketing Director, Pitspopany Press
        40 East 78th Street, Suite 16D
        New York, New York 10021
        Tel: 1-800-232-2931
        Fax: (212) 472-6253
        E-mail: pop@netvision.net.il
        Web: www.pitspopany.com

ISBN: 0-943706-45-9 Cloth
ISBN: 0-943706-49-1 Softcover

Printed in Hong Kong

Author's Note

Rebbe Nachman of Bratslav, 1772-1810, is revered as one of the greatest teachers of Judaism.

The Rooster Prince is based on a story by Rebbe Nachman who explained that in the same way as the hero of our story pretends to become a rooster in order to show the Prince how to become a man, so too the Tzaddik (sage or teacher) must go down to the spiritual level of the people if he is to raise them to new heights.

Along with this great Rebbe's tale, **The Rooster Prince** integrated the true story of my father, who as a young boy living near Kaminska, walked miles before Shabbat to the town shochet.

THE
ROOSTER
PRINCE

"A TERRIBLE FATE has befallen the son of the Tsar!" bellowed the Tsar's messenger.

"THE PRINCE THINKS HE IS A ROOSTER!"

Avron knew he should be hurrying home for Shabbat. Mother and Father were waiting for the scrawny chicken dangling by his side. Still, he couldn't resist seeing the Tsar's messenger and his shiny horse.

"The Prince gobbles, pecks and crows like a common rooster," continued the messenger.

"The Tsar offers a fine reward to anyone who can cure the Prince. Who amongst you knows about roosters or madness?"

The villagers of Kaminska tried not to laugh, "A Rooster Prince. Crazy! Meshuga!"

"The Tsar beheaded the last man who tried to save the Prince," whispered the Baker.

"What did the Tsar ever do for us?" asked the tailor, turning to go.

"Mother and Father are waiting for this Shabbat chicken," said Avron.

But before Avron could even leave the town square, the Tsar's messenger scooped him up like a sack of potatoes.

"I cannot return empty-handed or the Tsar will have my head. You carry chickens around with you. You must know about chickens and roosters."

The fields turned into a dusty blur of green grass and blue sky. Hooves thudded like thunder. Struggling to catch his breath, Avron barely managed to keep a grip on the chicken.

Dust settled as the horse's gallop turned into a trot.

Huge palace gates parted and then clanged shut. The echo struck Avron's heart with fear.

Tugged through the palace and into the gardens beyond, Avron wobbled as though he were walking on spindly chicken legs. There, amidst the blooms, was the Prince. His royal mouth was dark with dirt as he clawed at the roots of roses. The Tsar and Tsarina hovered around the Prince, shouting. Avron strained to listen.

"Leave this peasant game for the poor." The Tsar screamed, "You are to be the next Tsar, King of all."

"It must be a sorcerer's spell," the Tsarina moaned, throwing more grain to her son. The Prince kept gobbling his food, while flapping pretend feathers.

The Tzar paced back and forth.

"Russia needs a future ruler. Stand up straight!" he ordered.

But the Prince just bent lower, bobbing his head.

"Ah," said the Tsarina when she saw Avron. "This wise man will explain why this terrible fate has befallen us."

"Who cares why!" the Tsar yelled. "I want this crazy rooster turned into my son again. Bring this wise man before me now!" The messenger pushed Avron forward.

The Tsar scowled, "What can you know of madness? You are just a boy."

"Yes," said Avron, hoping the Tsar would send him home in time for Shabbat. "I am a simple boy, with no powers."

The Tsar scanned Avron from top to bottom, settling on the chicken. "You are well acquainted with chickens. Roosters, chickens. They are all the same family."

"I-I was just returning from the *shochet* with our Friday-night ch-chicken," stammered Avron.

"The *shochet*?"

"The special man who kills ch-chickens painlessly according to our holy law."

The Tsar waved his hand as if waving away Avron's words. "You will cure my son."

Avron quivered, "I-I don't know...."

"You know all about chickens, even how to kill them. You must know about roosters too."

"Your Majesty, it is Friday. Shabbat, our holy day, will begin at sundown. I must...."

"You must cure the Prince!" boomed the Tsar.

"Wh-what if I can't?"

"Hah!" An odd smile cracked the Tsar's stiff face. He signalled the messenger to snatch Avron's chicken. "Then you will never be hungry for a chicken again." Swinging his cape, the Tsar marched into the palace. His servants rushed to follow him.

Avron was left alone with the Prince. The Prince strutted along the garden paths pecking at roses and lilacs. Edging closer to Avron, he pushed his elbows up and out like bellows and snapped them close to his side. He squawked into Avron's face,

"CoCKADoODLeDoO!"

"You really are crazy," Avron said, burying his head in his hands.

Mother and Father would be worried beyond words.

Avron blinked and blinked hoping this was a bad dream; but the Prince and the gardens did not disappear. "Why are you pretending to be a bird?" Avron pleaded, "Your stupid game could cost me my life."

"CoCKADoODLEDoO!" The Prince called.

"CoCKaDooDLeDoo to you!" shouted Avron. His crowing seemed to delight the Prince who plopped grains at Avron's feet.

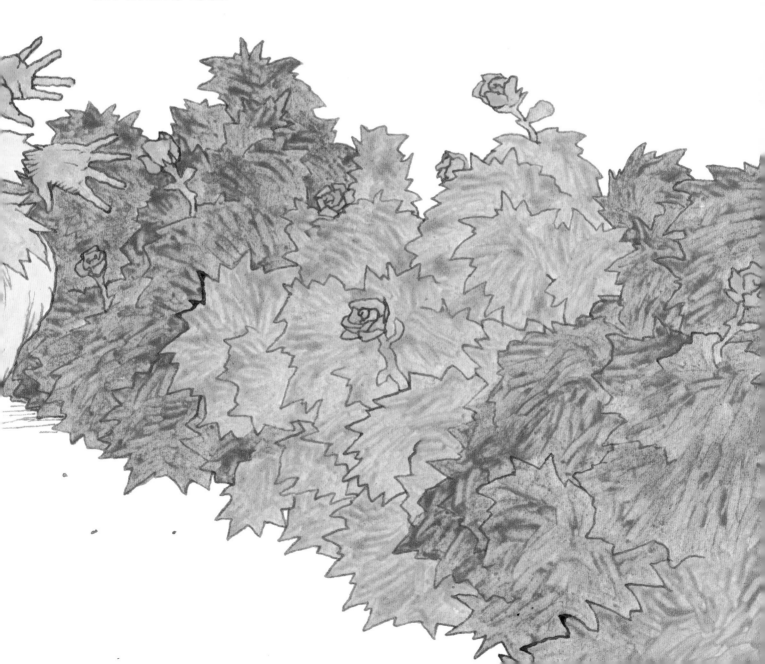

"He wants a friend," thought Avron. "Maybe if I pretend to be a rooster friend to the Prince, the Tsar will let me live." So Avron leaned down and pecked at the grains. They tasted dry and hard.

Tears trickled down Avron's dirty cheeks. Would he have to live all his days like this, on his haunches, pretending to be a rooster? Avron had often wished he could just have a glimpse of these beautiful gardens. Now, the shrubs seemed dark and dingy.

The Prince strutted closer to his new friend, and watched as Avron wiped his tears. The Prince wiped away his own pretend tears.

Avron's eyes widened with interest. He dried his eyes again. The Prince also wiped his eyes. Avron stretched his neck out and in like a rooster. The Prince mimicked him.

"CocKaDooDleDoo!" crowed Avron.

The Prince beamed at Avron and squawked,

"CoCKADoODLeDoO!"

Springing up, Avron waved his hands, calling the messenger.

"I know how to cure the Prince! I know how to cure the Prince!"

In the throne room, the Tsar's icy stare shot through Avron like winter's frost. "So, you say you can cure my son. Come closer," commanded the Tsar, "and tell me this secret."

"We have to..." Avron whispered. But before Avron could finish, the Tsar

stiffened and stared at him. The glare made Avron feel like a garden bug, but he tried to sound brave. "My Tsar, it has already worked."

The Tsar puckered his lips. Without taking his eyes off Avron, he nodded to his guards, "Get this boy whatever he needs. He's going to cure my son."

The next day Avron removed almost all his clothes and put them on the pile of clothes the servants had left for the Prince.

The Prince circled around Avron as though he wanted to play games. Ignoring the Prince, Avron just wobbled and squawked.

The Prince shadowed his new friend. Together they dug in the earth, nibbled corn and crowed to the garden gates.

"Are you a rooster too?" the Prince finally asked.

"Yes," said Avron,
  "A fine, special rooster."

Then the sun started to set and a chill blew over the blooms. Avron put on pants and a shirt. When completely clothed, he went back to his rooster stance.

The Prince made a squishy face, "Roosters don't wear clothes!"

"Why not?" asked Avron. "No need to be cold, just because I am a rooster. I am a smart rooster. A fine, special, rooster." Avron thrust his neck out and in.

The Prince moved closer to the clothes. He pulled out a pair of blue pants. He looked back and forth, from Avron to the pants. "How can you be a rooster and wear pants?"

"Of course I can. Russia is a cold country. I am a smart rooster."

The Prince glared at Avron while shaking the pants. Then in one fell swoop, he pulled the pants over his legs.

Avron breathed a long sigh of relief. Maybe, if his plan kept working, he would live to see his beloved mother and father.

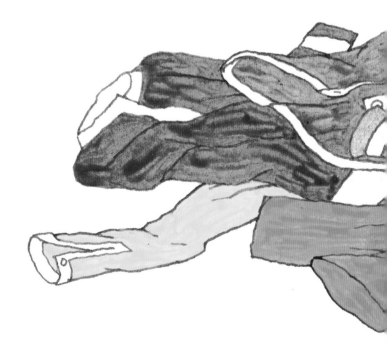

The next day, servants set platters of food on the ground. Smelling the potato piroshki and kasha made Avron's mouth water. Pecking like a rooster, he nibbled the delicacies.

With narrowing eyes, the Prince spit out the words, "Roosters can't eat that."

"Just because I'm a rooster doesn't mean I can't eat fine food," Avron said.

Smacking his lips together, the Prince watched Avron eat. Then he slowly moved towards the plate. He pecked at the kasha, before darting away. From a distance, he glared at Avron, his mouth watering with want. Then he skittered towards the food. Using his hands, he stuffed piroshki and kasha down his throat.

The next day Avron walked into the garden but did not stoop down. Instead he sat upright at the table filled with food. The Prince, now dressed and eating human food, looked up from under the table. "Humph. You are a rooster. You have to come down here," he insisted.

"Oh no," said Avron. "I am a fine, special rooster. I can stand. I can even sit at a table."

After a moment, the Prince stood up and sauntered over to a seat. He munched herring, vegetables and cakes. Avron's heart felt as full as his glass. Behind him the flowers glistened as if they had just burst into bloom.

So it was that the Prince returned to being a well-dressed, Russian-talking Prince. Except for the occasional,

"CᴏCKADᴏODLᴇDᴏO!"

all his rooster ways disappeared. The Tsarina no longer cared why he had pretended to be a rooster. She and the Tsar were happy to have their son back.

As a reward, the Tsar gave Avron a wagon filled with chickens, and a purse overflowing with gold rubles. Guiding the horses, Avron set out for Kaminska.

The hooves CLOPPED, the chickens *SQUAWKED,* and the purse JINGLED as Avron sang his favorite Shabbat song.

As he approached, the entire village gathered. The children cheered. Avron's mother and father hugged and kissed him.

Together, they enjoyed many Shabbat dinners. With the glow of the candles beside him, Avron often told the tale of the Rooster Prince. At the end of the story, Avron crowed,

"CocKaDooDleDoo!"

THE MAGIC BICYCLE

To Tim
B.D.

To Archie
C.B.

Text copyright © 1995 by Berlie Doherty
Illustrations copyright © 1995 by Christian Birmingham

Published in the United States by Crown Publishers, Inc.,
a Random House company, 201 East 50th Street, New York, New York 10022.
Published in Great Britain by HarperCollins Publishers Ltd. in 1995.

CROWN is a trademark of Crown Publishers, Inc.

Manufactured in Italy

Library of Congress Cataloging-in-Publication Data
Doherty, Berlie.
The magic bicycle / by Berlie Doherty ; illustrated by Christian Birmingham.
p. cm.
Simultaneously published in London as: The magical bicycle.
Summary: A boy finds that he cannot ride his new bicycle during the day, only in his dreams at night, until one day he finally discovers the magic he needs to ride it in real life.
[1. Bicycles and bicycling—Fiction. 2. Dreams—Fiction.]
I. Birmingham, Christian, ill. II. Title. III. Title: Magical bicycle.
PZ7.D6947Mag   1995
[E]—dc20   94-42116

ISBN 0-517-70902-3 (trade)
0-517-70903-1 (lib. bdg.)

10 9 8 7 6 5 4 3 2 1

First U.S. Edition

THE MAGIC BICYCLE

To Tim
B.D.

To Archie
C.B.

Text copyright © 1995 by Berlie Doherty
Illustrations copyright © 1995 by Christian Birmingham

Published in the United States by Crown Publishers, Inc.,
a Random House company, 201 East 50th Street, New York, New York 10022.
Published in Great Britain by HarperCollins Publishers Ltd. in 1995.

CROWN is a trademark of Crown Publishers, Inc.

Manufactured in Italy

Library of Congress Cataloging-in-Publication Data
Doherty, Berlie.
The magic bicycle / by Berlie Doherty ; illustrated by Christian Birmingham.
p. cm.
Simultaneously published in London as: The magical bicycle.
Summary: A boy finds that he cannot ride his new bicycle during the day, only in his dreams at night,
until one day he finally discovers the magic he needs to ride it in real life.
[1. Bicycles and bicycling—Fiction. 2. Dreams—Fiction.]
I. Birmingham, Christian, ill. II. Title. III. Title: Magical bicycle.
PZ7.D6947Mag   1995
[E]—dc20   94-42116

ISBN 0-517-70902-3 (trade)
0-517-70903-1 (lib. bdg.)

10 9 8 7 6 5 4 3 2 1

First U.S. Edition

THE MAGIC BICYCLE

by Berlie Doherty

illustrated by Christian Birmingham

CROWN PUBLISHERS, INC., *New York*

My best surprise
Was my shining bike
With its silver voice.
But I couldn't ride it.

Every time I tried it
Threw me off.
I think it thought
It was a horse.

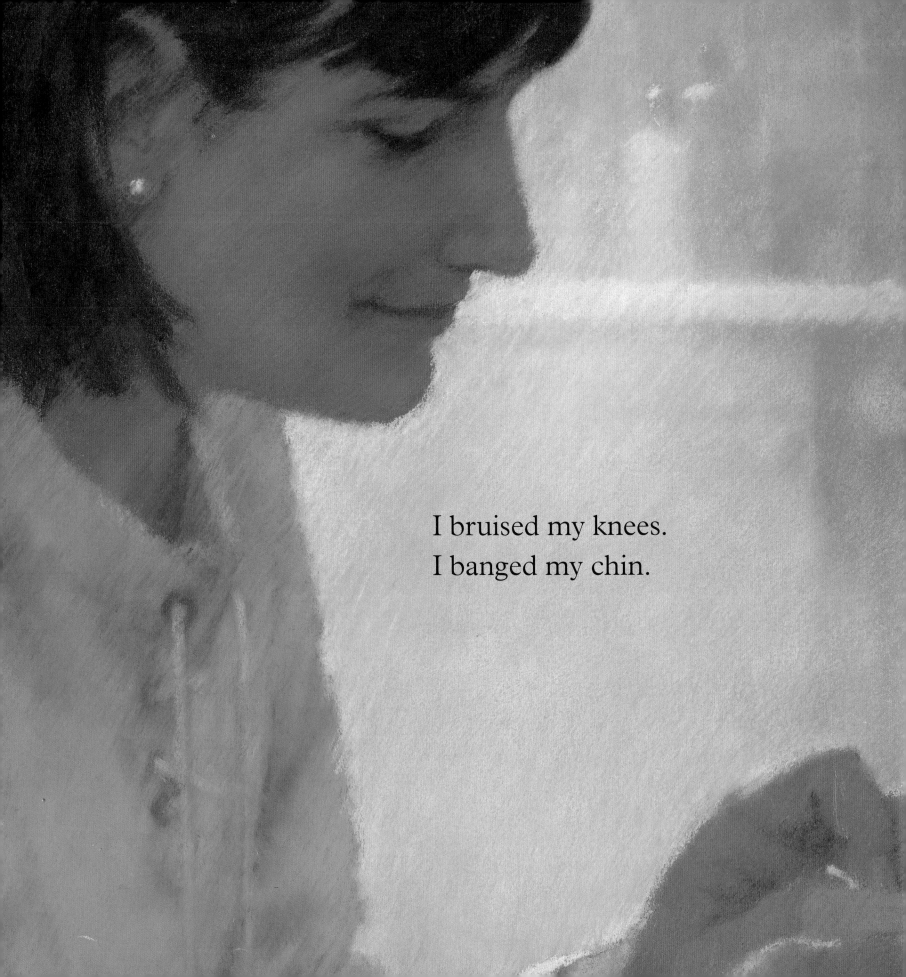

I bruised my knees.
I banged my chin.

I tried again, again, again.

My brother can glide it
Round and round.
Jenny can race it up and down.
Even my uncle can wobble astride it.
Everybody I know can ride it.

It must be something to do with magic.
There must be a special, secret trick.
There must be a spell on bikes, I decided.

Dad ran up the driveway, holding on.
And then he ran all the way down
And panted all the way up again.

"Just turn your legs!"
He grew tired and slow.
"You won't fall off..."

And I never did
Till he let go.

But every night, deep in my dreams,
I rode my bike
Over the trees,
As high as the birds,
Over the mountains,
Over the world.

And every day I tried again.
I gave my dad another chance.
"I WILL ride my bike!" I shouted out loud.

And I fell off.

I spat on my hands
And rubbed my knees.
I picked up my bike
And tried to look proud.

"It's just a matter of magic," I said.
"That's all it is."

And then one day,
I must have
Said it.
The magic word.
I didn't hear it.
I didn't think it.
It must have been
Deep in the quietest part of my mind.

There was Dad, running behind me,
I could hear his footsteps
Fainter and fainter.
I could feel the air
On my face and my hair.
I could feel my own power,
I could feel my own strength,
I could hear the wheels turning.
My legs were like pistons
And I knew I could do it,
I could cycle forever.

Like a bird over mountains,
Like a ship over oceans,
To the end of the world,
I had magic in me.